D1349696

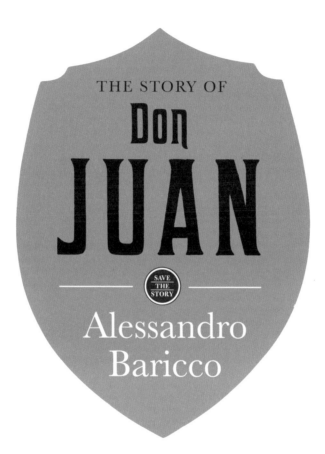

THE STORY OF
DON
JUAN

SAVE THE STORY

Alessandro Baricco

ILLUSTRATED BY
ALESSANDRO MARIA NACAR

Translated by Ann Goldstein

PUSHKIN CHILDREN'S BOOKS

Pushkin Children's Books
71–75 Shelton Street
London W C 2 H 9 J Q

The Story of Don Juan first published in Italian as *La storia di Don Giovanni*

This edition published by Pushkin Children's Books in 2013

ISBN 978 1 782690 15 3

Set in Garamond Premier Pro by Tetragon, London

Printed and bound in Italy by Printer Trento SRL
on Munken Print Cream 115gsm

www.pushkinpress.com

THE STORY OF
Don
JUAN

One

It all happened many years ago, in a beautiful light-filled city in southern Spain. In those days, men went about with swords, people rode on horseback and houses were lit by candles. No airplanes and no computers, just to be clear. The hours passed quickly: the poor worked hard, the rich thought about amusing themselves. They all had a will to live, and the magnificent city encouraged them to be happy: from afar came the smell of the sea, and trees weighed down with oranges brightened the streets.

Now, you must know that in that city lived a beautiful, wealthy girl whose name was Donn'Anna. She lived with her father, who was very powerful and very stern: Don Gonzalo de Ulloa, Commendatore of Calatrava. His name was so long that, to simplify things, everyone called him the Commendatore. In those days, fathers chose husbands for their daughters, and the Commendatore had chosen for his daughter a kind, gentle man, whom Donn'Anna had come to love: his name was Don Ottavio. They certainly would have married, and probably would have been happy, but one night something happened that changed their lives for ever.

It was, to be precise, a summer night, a lovely warm night. Donn'Anna was in her room, getting ready to go to sleep. The windows were open and a light breeze stirred the leaves on the trees in the garden. Everything is perfect, Donn'Anna thought. She blew out the candle and lay down on her bed. But suddenly she heard a noise outside, and when she turned she saw by the light of the moon a man wrapped in a large cloak entering through the window, with a grace that she immediately recognized: Don Ottavio, she thought. He's come to give me a secret goodnight kiss. "There, he's not as boring as everyone thinks," she said to herself. And she rose, happily, and went to meet him, and they embraced. The man kissed her passionately, and the odd thing was that in his arms Donn'Anna felt an emotion she had never felt before. She didn't understand why, but those kisses were so different, so new, so beautiful that she was almost frightened by them, and she opened her eyes to look for Don Ottavio's, and their sweetness. But she couldn't find them: the man wore a dark mask. And over his head a hood that covered him. "Don Ottavio!" said Donn'Anna. But the man said nothing, only sought to clasp her again, and kiss her. Then Donn'Anna stiffened, and said again, in a louder voice, "Don Ottavio!" Yet again the man didn't answer. Alarmed, Donn'Anna slipped out of his arms and cried, "Who are you? I don't know you. Who are you?" The man looked around, muttered something in a low voice and made as if to flee. Then Donn'Anna hurled herself at him, angrily, and with one hand tried to rip off the mask. "Who are you?" she cried, again and again.

"Who I am you will never know," the man answered, in an unfamiliar voice.

Donn'Anna stood motionless, stunned. She thought of those kisses, of those strong arms, of the lips of that man which had so thrilled her, and she felt she would die of shame and rage.

"Why did you do that?" she asked.

"Because you are so beautiful, my dear Donn'Anna," said the man.

He said it with a smile, with an impudence that made Donn'Anna blind with rage. "You villain!" she began to shout, grabbing at the man like a madwoman and trying to rip off his cloak and tear away that cursed mask. The man tried to hold her off, but she hung on, clinging to him even as he left the room, swearing, and ran down the staircase, looking for a way out. "You're crazy," he said to her in a low voice. "Be quiet or you'll wake the entire household." But she wouldn't stop shouting, between her tears, and clutching him, and trying to stop him. "You won't get away like this, you can't get away like this!" she cried, and she didn't care about the scandal, and the servants who would come out of their rooms or anyone else who found her like this, in tears, clinging to a man she didn't know. The only thing that mattered to her was to find out who that man was. For this reason, with a final effort and a final cry, she attacked his face with her hands and managed to touch the mask, and almost tear it off,

when in the empty darkness of the grand staircase she heard a voice, clear, deep and firm, which said, "Leave my daughter alone, immediately."

Her father, the Commendatore.

He was standing at the foot of the staircase, holding a sword in his hand.

The mysterious man stopped. Donn'Anna was silent, and took a few steps backwards. Then she ran up the stairs, to her room. Suddenly she felt all the fear, and the sorrow, and the shame for what had happened to her.

The two men stood face to face, unmoving. The old father and the young man with no name. They stared at each other. There was no one else, just the two of them. And the night. And that immense staircase.

"Don't make me draw my sword," said the young man.

"But you will, if you are not a coward," said the Commendatore.

"You're too old to fight me," said the young man.

"But not too old to kill you," said the Commendatore, and charged him. Quick as lightning, the masked man drew his sword, took a step back to avoid the old man's thrust, and then, with a rapid, precise gesture, plunged the sword into his breast. The Commendatore staggered, and fell to the ground. He tried to get up, but he couldn't find the strength. He understood that he was dying and, gathering all the forces that remained to him, said, in a low voice, "Who are you?"

The mysterious man leant over him. He gazed into his eyes. And he took off the mask. The Commendatore looked at that face for an instant, recognized it and thought that life was a difficult game, too difficult, for him and for everyone.

"Don Juan," he said faintly.

His head fell back, and he died.

Two

Never, ever had Don Juan killed a man. So he stood there, looking at that face which only a moment before had been alive and was now like stone. He would have continued to stare at it, in fascination, for quite a while, but he heard someone approaching, and he couldn't be discovered there, with the sword in his hand and the bloody corpse of the Commendatore. So he cast a last glance at the dead man, gave him a nod of farewell and hurried away.

Not that it was simple to escape without being seen, but, hiding here and there, climbing walls, and stealing silently through passageways, he finally got to the street, safe and sound. His servant was supposed to be around

somewhere; he had left him there, to
wait. So he began calling him.

"Leporello! Hey, Leporello!"

The servant emerged from a clump
of bushes. "Here I am, master. How
did it go?"

"It could have gone better."

"You found Donn'Anna?"

"Yes, but then it all got a bit
complicated. That girl has a temper..."

"You're not telling me that instead of calmly
letting you kiss her she started shouting!"

"Shouting and scratching and... well, she made
such a racket that in the end her father showed up."

"The Commendatore in person?"

"Yes. He showed up, drew his sword and
challenged me to a duel."

"A duel? Help! And who won?"

"Who do you think won, you idiot! Don't you
see me here, safe and sound?"

"And the Commendatore?"

"Dead."

"Dead?"

"Very dead."

"You killed him!"

"Definitely killed."

"Master, you just killed the Commendatore, one of the most powerful men in the city, and you're walking along the street here like this, as if it were nothing?"

"Well, he's the one that's dead, not me. I want to have some fun. In fact, let's go down to the river, you can meet certain girls there, I don't know if you've noticed, but the prettiest girls are always in that neighbourhood, along the river, at this time of night..."

"You're mad, master."

"Wrong: I'm alive, that's all."

"You don't care about anything. You've just killed a man and you're going around looking for girls—what sort of heart do you have?"

"A big heart, obviously, dear Leporello. Too big to love only Donn'Anna, however beautiful she is; too big to be sad because of an old

man who died a little earlier than expected; too big to go on listening to your boring sermons when there's the whole city having fun on this beautiful night, and just waiting for me. In fact, look down there—doesn't it seem to you that she's waiting for me?"

"Who? That woman?"

"Precisely," said Don Juan. "She seems sad, she's walking slowly, she's looking around as if she's lost. Let's go see."

"Master, forget it, maybe she's just waiting for her lover."

"Exactly. Let's go and save her right now."

"Save her? I know how you save women."

"Silence! Leave it to me. Signorina! Signorina!"

She was a very elegant, very beautiful woman, it should be said. She heard that voice calling her and so she looked up. At first she couldn't understand where the voice was coming from, but again she heard "Signorina!" and then she turned and saw that man, very gallantly making a slight bow. She observed him carefully. She couldn't believe her eyes. She knew that man. She had travelled across all Spain to find that man. She wanted to kill that man.

"What the devil, that's Donna Elvira," said Leporello.

"I can't believe it! It's her all right," said Don Juan.

"You, you coward!" the woman cried.

"She's recognized you," said Leporello.

"Don Juan, I'll kill you!" the woman said, more specifically.

It was, in fact, Donna Elvira, a noblewoman who was usually sweet and kind, but not that night, and the reason is quickly explained. Months earlier, in another city in Spain, Don Juan had courted her for a long time, then had ravished her, made her fall in love with him, and finally married her, promising eternal love. The next day, however, he had run off and hadn't been seen again. Not a word, not an explanation, nothing. From that day, Donna Elvira had been searching for him. She had travelled miles and miles, following his tracks, always with the hope of one day finding him. What she would do that day was very clear to her: she would murder him. And now that day had arrived. That man was before her. On a summer night she had found the man who ruined her and she could finally tell him what she thought of him.

"I love you," she said.

"See?" said Don Juan to Leporello. "Nothing to worry about."

"I love you very much," said Donna Elvira, "but now I'm going to kill you."

Three

In fact she didn't kill him: it didn't happen exactly like that. In fact they began to talk, which at times, however, is even worse than killing. Donna Elvira wanted to know why: why Don Juan had fled, why he had married her if he didn't want to stay with her, why he was so handsome, so lovable, and a bastard.

"You explain it," said Don Juan to his servant, Leporello.

"Me?"

"Yes, you, you know everything. Show her the catalogue."

"No, the catalogue no, that I really can't do."

"But I order you: show her the catalogue."

"Catalogue?" said Donna Elvira, her curiosity roused. Don Juan went up to her and gently took her hands. He told her that, unfortunately, he really had to go, he had a very urgent appointment, but she mustn't worry, Leporello would explain

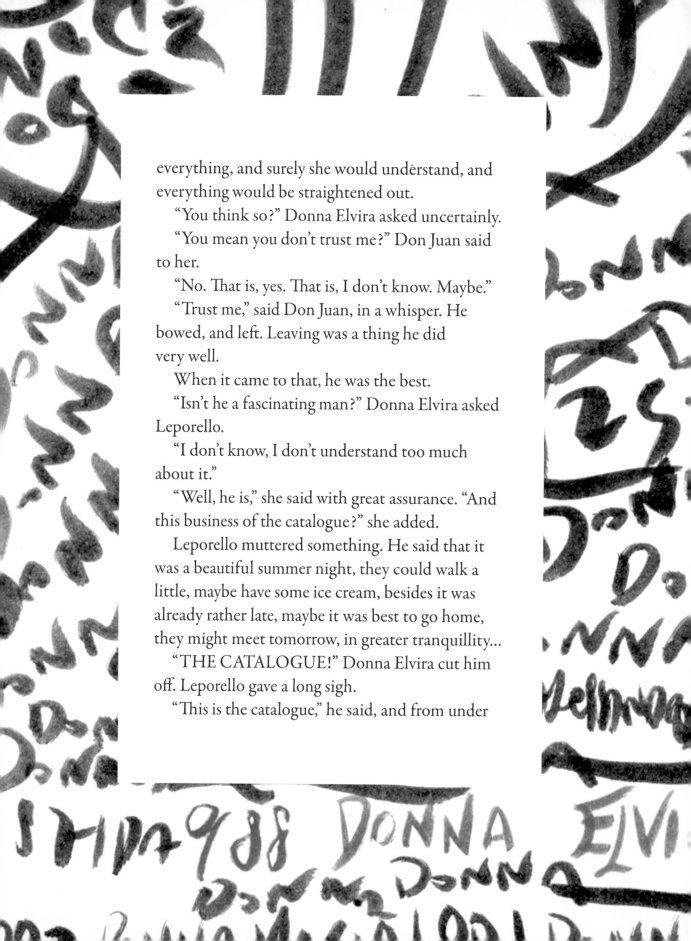

everything, and surely she would understand, and everything would be straightened out.

"You think so?" Donna Elvira asked uncertainly.

"You mean you don't trust me?" Don Juan said to her.

"No. That is, yes. That is, I don't know. Maybe."

"Trust me," said Don Juan, in a whisper. He bowed, and left. Leaving was a thing he did very well.

When it came to that, he was the best.

"Isn't he a fascinating man?" Donna Elvira asked Leporello.

"I don't know, I don't understand too much about it."

"Well, he is," she said with great assurance. "And this business of the catalogue?" she added.

Leporello muttered something. He said that it was a beautiful summer night, they could walk a little, maybe have some ice cream, besides it was already rather late, maybe it was best to go home, they might meet tomorrow, in greater tranquillity...

"THE CATALOGUE!" Donna Elvira cut him off. Leporello gave a long sigh.

"This is the catalogue," he said, and from under

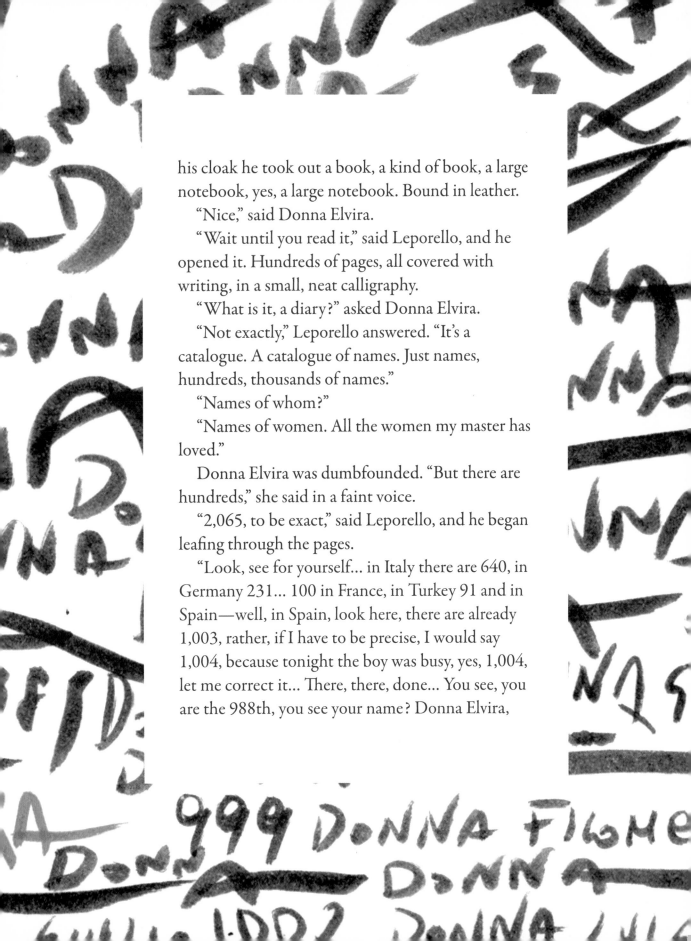

his cloak he took out a book, a kind of book, a large notebook, yes, a large notebook. Bound in leather.

"Nice," said Donna Elvira.

"Wait until you read it," said Leporello, and he opened it. Hundreds of pages, all covered with writing, in a small, neat calligraphy.

"What is it, a diary?" asked Donna Elvira.

"Not exactly," Leporello answered. "It's a catalogue. A catalogue of names. Just names, hundreds, thousands of names."

"Names of whom?"

"Names of women. All the women my master has loved."

Donna Elvira was dumbfounded. "But there are hundreds," she said in a faint voice.

"2,065, to be exact," said Leporello, and he began leafing through the pages.

"Look, see for yourself... in Italy there are 640, in Germany 231... 100 in France, in Turkey 91 and in Spain—well, in Spain, look here, there are already 1,003, rather, if I have to be precise, I would say 1,004, because tonight the boy was busy, yes, 1,004, let me correct it... There, there, done... You see, you are the 988th, you see your name? Donna Elvira, number 988, it's all done in a very orderly fashion, you know?"

Donna Elvira looked at it in astonishment. Leporello realized that he had better explain things a little more clearly. He had the tone of someone who is explaining how a light bulb works. Or a computer. Something like that.

"You see," he said, "my master likes them all, and I mean all. Peasant girls, servant girls, city girls, countesses, baronesses, marchionesses, princesses; he doesn't care if they're rich or poor, young or old—in each of them he finds something, something extraordinary. He likes blondes, he says they're kind, but dark-haired girls will do very well, too, dark-haired girls have character, he always says. In winter he likes fat girls, to keep him warm, in summer he prefers them thin, so he doesn't sweat... He'll even court old women, grandmothers, just for the pleasure of expanding his collection, you know? even though, unquestionably, he prefers the young ones, the very young, they're the ones who make him go wild, the beginners... He's like that, and there's nothing to be done about it: they can be pretty, ugly, big, small, intelligent, stupid, it makes no difference—if they're women he loves them. And if they're women, believe me, they love him. Do you think you understand now?"

Donna Elvira kept her gaze fixed on the book. Maybe her legs trembled a little, but it was hard to say, they couldn't be seen, concealed as they were under that long and very stylish cloak. When she spoke, she spoke in a firm voice, without any sadness.

"I fell in love with an imbecile."

"Not at all," Leporello protested. "Don't come to that conclusion. Don Juan isn't an imbecile, he's just a man who loves women, and he loves them so much that it's impossible for him to love one alone. He's so kind that he couldn't disappoint even one, and if they want him why should he hold back? Think about it: he made you suffer, it's true, but it was to make another happy—many others. If he had stayed with you, married, in slippers, with a string of brats under his feet, how many other women would not have known happiness, and the taste of life and freedom that only he can provide? You yourself—would you ever have known him if he had married the one before you? Tell me, all in all, what would you prefer? A single day of happiness with him, in

29

your whole life, or a whole life without ever having met him?"

Donna Elvira knew exactly how to answer: "I would prefer a whole life of happiness with him."

"But that's impossible!" said Leporello. "He loves life and freedom too much to put them in the hands of a single woman—that he'll never do. And I'll tell you something else: none of us would, we men, if only we had his courage, his daring and his pride. Believe me."

Donna Elvira looked at him.

"You like him, your master," she said.

"Oh no, I don't mean that, he's a wicked man, and sooner or later he'll be punished, certainly, someone will make him pay, but..."

"But you like him," Donna Elvira repeated.

"Maybe. A little. Every so often. And you?"

Donna Elvira smiled.

"I must thank you, Leporello," she said. "You've taught me many things, and all in one night. Now I know what I must do."

"Really?" Leporello asked, rather proud of himself. It was the first time a noblewoman had spoken to him like that.

"Yes, really," said Donna Elvira. "Tell Don Juan that he doesn't have to worry about me, I'll let him live in peace with his freedom and his courage. Tell him that I forgive him, and that as far as I'm concerned I'll just try to forget him."

Then she smiled, a beautiful smile, like an angel's.

"As for killing him, in fact, my brothers will take care of that," she said.

Four

"Brothers?" Don Juan asked the next morning when Leporello told him everything. "Donna Elvira has brothers?"

While he was helping him dress, Leporello explained that there were two brothers, and it seemed that they were arriving on horseback, accompanied by ten swordsmen. That made twelve in all. Too many to think of fighting. So the possibilities were two: either flee at once or stay and be chopped into tiny pieces by a band of fierce, bloodthirsty assassins.

"I think I'll choose the first," Don Juan said, as he was putting on his boots.

"Excellent choice," said Leporello, who had two horses ready at the front door.

They went off like rockets—rockets didn't exist at the time, of course, but just so you understand. The plan was to leave the city and hide for a while in some country town. Except that at a certain point, as they were crossing a square, Don Juan saw a funeral procession coming out of a church, and it made him curious, so curious that he stopped. Leporello yelled at him to get moving, they were wasting time, but he just sat there for a while, watching, as if he were looking for something. And finally he must have found it, because he dismounted from his horse and, handing the reins to Leporello, said:

"Wait for me, I have to see someone."

"Master, does it really seem to you the right moment to go to a funeral?"

"It's not any funeral, Leporello. We know the dead man."

"We do?"

"Take a close look," said Don Juan, and he headed towards the church. Leporello took a close look. He saw something that he would have preferred not to see.

"That's the Commendatore," he said in a voice trembling with fear. "It's the funeral of the Commendatore! Master, let's get out of here, please!" he started shouting.

But Don Juan could no longer hear him, for by now he was near the church and, making his way through the crowd, had reached Donn'Anna. She was on Don Ottavio's arm, richly clothed in black, her eyes hidden by a veil; her skin was very white, and her carmine-red lips shone brightly against it. People went up to her one by one, to offer their respects and condolences: she smiled, sadly, at everyone, with great refinement. Finally it was Don Juan's turn. He stopped in front of Don Ottavio, greeting him with a brief bow. Then he turned to Donn'Anna.

"I imagine what you must have suffered, that night," he said. "But be assured, your father will sooner or later be avenged."

She nodded politely and gave him her hand.

He leant over and touched it with his lips, in a very courteous, chaste manner. But as he straightened up he stared into her eyes and in a low voice said, with a sigh, "You may count on me—I would do anything for you, beautiful Donn'Anna." And then he vanished into the crowd, like lightning. As I said: leaving was the thing he did best.

Not a moment had passed before Donn'Anna turned to Don Ottavio and asked him softly, "Who was that man?"

"It's Don Juan, a count, I think, who arrived in the city a short time ago."

She trembled. She clung even more tightly to Don Ottavio's arm and said, "It's he. It's he who killed my father. I recognized him."

"But Don Juan is a gentleman, it can't have been he," said Don Ottavio.

"I tell you it's he."

"How do you know?" asked Don Ottavio.

"That way of looking at me. And the voice. And the lips. It's he."

"Lips?" asked Don Ottavio in surprise. "What do you know about his lips?"

Donn'Anna looked him in the eye.

"Do you really want to know?" she asked.

"I'm not sure," he said.

Donn'Anna smiled at him. She was no longer pale as before. She turned towards the square, just in time to see Don Juan disappearing at a gallop into a narrow street.

"Now that you know who is guilty, will you avenge me?" she asked Don Ottavio.

Don Ottavio was a calm man, even a little too calm. "I was thinking, rather, of going to the police to report him," he answered. To him it seemed a good response.

Donn'Anna looked at him as she would have looked at a sock that fell from the sky into her soup.

"Be careful not to hurt yourself," she said.

Five

In the open countryside, far from the
city, Don Juan and Leporello, mounted
on their horses, were proceeding at
a walk in the warm afternoon light.

To keep them from growing bored,
Leporello was recounting how things
had gone with Donna Elvira the night
before: the whole story of the catalogue.
Don Juan found it very amusing. What
made him laugh above all was the
point where Leporello began to read all
those numbers and Donna Elvira stood
listening, like a statue.

He found it irresistible. Too bad he hadn't been there. On the other hand, he said to Leporello, escaping had allowed him to find in the night a woman with whom he had really enjoyed himself.

"Another adventure to add to the catalogue?" asked Leporello.

"Exactly. Go ahead and add it."

"Old or young?"

"Very young."

"Dark?"

"Blonde."

"Nice?"

"Very nice."

"Rich or poor?"

"A servant girl."

"Did you have to promise to marry her?"

"No need."

"You mean she opened her arms without asking anything in exchange?"

"Not a thing. She did it out of passion."

"Good heavens, I'd like to know her, too."

"But you do know her, Leporello."

"Really?"

"Small, with blue eyes, two pretty dimples when she smiles…"

"And she speaks very quickly?" asked Leporello.

"Exactly."

"Has a little brother who's always in the way?"

"Exactly."

"And a father always drunk at the Golden Lion?"

"Exactly."

"Barberina!"

"Exactly."

Leporello stopped his horse.

"But she's my betrothed," he said.

"I compliment you on your choice," said Don Juan.

"YOU ARE A MONSTER!" Leporello shouted, and spurred his horse, but Don Juan was already off into the countryside, laughing as hard as he could.

They galloped like that for minutes, with Leporello yelling and Don Juan laughing, and they would never have stopped if, at a certain point, as they came around a low hill, they hadn't seen on the road ahead a gentleman who, assaulted by three brigands, was trying to defend himself with his sword.

"One against three, that's not fair," Don Juan observed, stopping his horse.

"DON'T CHANGE THE SUBJECT!" Leporello yelled, even more enraged.

"SILENCE!" Don Juan ordered. Then he unsheathed his sword and said, "Let's see about doing our duty instead." And he took off at a gallop.

He fell on the three brigands with such rapidity and dealing such thrusts of the sword that they first wondered what was happening and then decided that it was better to get out of it. They turned their horses and disappeared into the countryside.

"God sent you," said the gentleman who had been assaulted, heaving a great sigh of relief.

"God?" said Don Juan. "I don't think so—it's a long time since He and I have kept company."

"Be that as it may, you saved my life, sir," the gentleman continued. "Allow me to introduce myself: my name is Don Carlo. I was with my brother and ten other swordsmen, but I was delayed and then I lost my way. You see, if I may confide in you, we are going to the city to kill a man."

"Really?" said Don Juan.

"A villain, a monster, an assassin. He seduced our

sister, married her and then vanished into thin air. But now we have discovered where he's hiding. And you may be sure that this time he won't escape."

"What's this man's name?" Leporello asked.

"His name is Don Juan," answered Don Carlo.

"Ah," said Don Juan.

"You know him?" asked Don Carlo.

"By sight," said Don Juan. "I happened to dine with him."

Don Carlo appeared to be interested.

"Is it true that he's so fascinating? You know, I've never even seen him, this Don Juan."

"Oh, well, I think you'll see him soon," said Don Juan. "In fact, very soon." And he made as if to draw his sword.

"Well, it's late," Leporello interrupted. He couldn't wait to get out of there. "Now we really have to be going."

Don Juan gave him a withering look, and God knows what he would have done, but just at that moment, on the crest of the hill, a group of horsemen appeared.

"Look! Don Alfonso, my brother!" said Don Carlo, elated.

47

The horsemen descended through the fields and in a moment were beside them. The one who was obviously their leader stopped his horse just in front of Don Juan. He stared at him. Then, without turning, he asked Don Carlo, in a loud voice:

"Brother, whom are you talking to?"

"A noble soul who just saved my life," Don Carlo answered.

"Wrong. With a worthless soul who ruined your sister's life."

Don Carlo was dumbfounded.

"Don Juan?" he stammered.

"At your service," said Don Juan, with a bow. All together, instantaneously, the ten swordsmen drew their swords.

Six

They would have killed him, certainly they would have killed him. They were ten, plus that brother, Don Alfonso, who seemed the fiercest of them all. For Don Juan it was truly over, this time. He drew his sword, more as a stylish gesture than for anything else, and he hoped that maybe a meteorite would fall from the sky and hit them squarely, all except him and Leporello.

There weren't many possibilities, agreed, but being an optimist was another thing that he was very good at. So he glanced up at the sky; you never know. He was verifying that there wasn't a cloud, still less a meteorite, when he heard the voice of Don Carlo shouting:

"Stop!"

The ten swordsmen, plus Don Alfonso, were ready, swords unsheathed, to stab Don Juan. They turned to Don Carlo in amazement.

"Stop?"

"This man just saved my life," said Don Carlo. "If you attack him I will be compelled to defend him."

"Why?" they asked, in chorus.

"What do you mean, why? He saved my life, don't you get it? And I should stand here watching you cut him to pieces without lifting a finger? I mean, what sort of people are you?" He seemed quite angry, Don Carlo did.

Then his brother Alfonso went up to him, and spoke in a very calm, soft voice.

"Dear brother," he said, "you really are a noble man, and I admire the loyalty that has dictated these remarkable words. I'm moved." He turned to the ten swordsmen. "We're all moved, aren't we?" he asked.

The ten swordsmen sniffed, showing themselves to be very moved.

"Good," he continued. "And now that we are moved, we come to the point. This man seduced our sister, befuddled her with his nauseating sweet talk, persuaded her to marry him and the next morning disappeared, without even paying the bill at the inn. For three months, I tell you three months, I've been sitting on this horse, looking for this outlaw through all Spain, and now I've finally found him. We are twelve against one, and there is no probability in the world that this man can escape. And so, little brother, I will be brief: get out of the way, because now I'm going to kill him."

"You won't!" cried Don Carlo.

"Yes I will!" cried Don Alfonso.

"No you won't!" cried Don Carlo.

"I certainly will!" cried Don Alfonso.

"Try it!" cried Don Carlo.

"I'm trying," cried Don Alfonso.

"May I say something?" said Don Juan.

They all turned to him.

"Excuse me if I'm intruding, but I have a solution," said Don Juan.

They were all silent, waiting.

"You see, it's evident that you, Don Alfonso, are fully entitled to cut me to pieces. On the other hand, you, too, are correct, dear Don Carlo, to claim that this should not happen before your eyes, since you owe your life to me. All right. Let's do this: let me live for another twenty-four hours, twenty-four hours only, and I will consider it a gift from Don Carlo, who will thus, in turn, have saved my life. In twenty-four hours you will find me in my house, in the city, and then you will be free, all of you, to do what you like with me. I swear to you that I will be there, alone as I am now, and at your disposition. I swear it on my honour."

There was a long moment of silence. They were all wondering where the catch was. But nothing came to mind.

"Twenty-four hours, not one more?" asked Don Alfonso.

"I swear it," said Don Juan.

"And in this way I will have squared my debt with you?" asked Don Carlo.

"You may be sure of it," answered Don Juan.

It seemed in effect a good solution. They all lowered their swords.

"So in twenty-four hours, at your house, in the city," said Don Alfonso.

"I'll be there," said Don Juan.

"I hope so, for your sake," said Don Alfonso, and, turning his horse, he galloped off. Don Carlo followed him and then the ten swordsmen. They disappeared over the horizon. Don Juan and

Leporello stood there, in the countryside, in the half-light of evening.

"I can't believe it," said Leporello, heaving a long sigh of relief. "We're still alive."

"For twenty-four hours," said Don Juan.

"Are you joking? You're not telling me that in twenty-four hours you're going to be there? We're going to flee as far away as possible now, right?"

Don Juan looked him in the eye.

"I've given my word," he said. "Tomorrow evening I'll be in my house, alone, waiting for them."

"You're a dead man," said Leporello. Don Juan smiled.

"Not yet, Leporello, not yet," he said.

Seven

So they returned to the city, Leporello
muttering and Don Juan silent,
sunk in his thoughts. It was dark
when they came in sight of the walls,
where the road passed by a cemetery.

The moon was so big that it lit up the
tombs and made them seem whiter and
more spectral than ever.

They gazed in silence at that strange sight, and
at a certain point they saw an enormous, extremely
ornate tomb that they had never noticed before.

There was even a statue of the dead man, and the dead man was on horseback, and everything was as big as if it were real.

"Truly impressive," Don Juan said. "Leporello, go and see who has made such a monument for himself."

Leporello had no wish to go into the cemetery, but he got off his horse and approached the tomb. He leant over to read the stone, where the name of the dead man was. He jumped back and let out a cry.

"So?" asked Don Juan.

"Let's get out of here," Leporello said, his voice full of fear.

"Read that tombstone!" Don Juan ordered.

"I can't read in the moonlight..."

"Read it, I order you!"

So, in spite of his terror, Leporello again approached the tomb and began to read. His voice trembled and he could barely get the words out, he was so frightened.

"Here lies buried... Don Gonzalo de Ulloa, Commendatore of Calatrava. Here... he awaits his revenge... and the punishment of the impious man who killed him."

"The Commendatore!" Don Juan said gaily. "There's no getting that old man out from under our feet." And he began to laugh, but hard, really a hearty laugh.

Before a moment had passed they heard in the air a mournful voice. It spoke slowly, as if it were making a tremendous effort. But what it said could be understood very clearly.

"RESPECT THE PEACE OF THE DEAD, IMPIOUS MAN. OR YOU WILL STOP LAUGHING BEFORE THIS NIGHT IS THROUGH."

"Master!" cried Leporello. "The statue speaks!"

Don Juan didn't lose his composure.

"So it seems, Leporello. It's a truly strange spectacle."

"Master, master, let's get out of here!"

"Why? A statue that wants to speak doesn't turn up every day. In fact, you know what, I like him: tell him that I'm inviting him to dinner, at my house, tomorrow night."

"To dinner? A statue? You tell him!" said Leporello.

"Don't talk back to me or I'll murder you and bury you here. Go on, invite the statue to dinner!"

Leporello was terrified. But what could he do? He took a step towards the statue and, trying to keep his eyes on it, said slowly:

"Most honourable statue of Sir Commendatore... my master, not I, take note, but my master humbly asks if by chance, however absurd... I can't do it, master!"

"Go on, or I'll murder you and bury you here," cried Don Juan, who was really beginning to be amused.

"My master," Leporello continued, "very humbly invites you to dine with him, tomorrow night, at his house. He would be honoured if you would accept. On the other hand you can also say no, he won't be absolutely insulted."

Don Juan was enjoying the scene. "Ask if it will come," he ordered Leporello.

Leporello was so frightened that he had no voice left in his throat. But still he managed to find a last ounce of courage to look at the statue and say:

"Speak, if you can, and tell us: will you come to dinner?"

Then a really incredible thing happened: the head of the statue moved, downward, and nodded yes, three times. The head of the statue, as if it were alive.

"Truly amazing," said Don Juan. "The good old fellow will come to dinner. What he

wouldn't do to scrounge a meal. Excellent. Let's see that we welcome him with all the magnificence he deserves. Let's go, Leporello, we have to organize a proper feast." And he spurred his horse to a trot, in the direction of the city.

Leporello said nothing for a while. His teeth were chattering from the shock, and he couldn't stop them. He was riding behind Don Juan, thinking over what he had seen. It took him a moment to recover his composure, and say what was buzzing around in his head.

"Master... apart from the fact that you invited a statue to eat, and I want to see what you'll put on his plate—marble cutlets? Stone meatballs? Apart from that, didn't it occur to you that you're busy tomorrow evening?"

"Busy, me?" Don Juan pretended not to understand.

"Nothing much," said Leporello. "You only promised to have yourself murdered at your house by two furious brothers and ten bloodthirsty swordsmen."

"Ah, that," said Don Juan. "No problem, they'll wait."

"Wait? They've been waiting for three months!"

"It means we'll invite them to dinner, too. You kill better on a full stomach."

Leporello was astonished. He thought he knew his master, but such calm, such courage, was really surprising.

"Master," he said, "have you ever been afraid of anything?"

Don Juan was well acquainted with that question.

"Only of being bored," he answered.

Eight

Don Juan spent the next day in preparations. He did things in a big way. Two cooks, twelve serving men, silver plates and cutlery, an orchestra, the choicest wines and candles everywhere, illuminating the house as if it were day. Marvellous. He was in a very good mood and wasn't even bothered when Leporello arrived, panting, in the middle of the afternoon, bringing bad news.

He said that he had enquired and had learnt that Don Ottavio, the betrothed of Donn'Anna, had gone to the police. He had said he had discovered who the assassin of the Commendatore was: who knows how, but he'd got it right, and had accused Don Juan.

The police had believed him and now were organizing. That night, at sunset, dozens of

soldiers would arrive there, at the house, to arrest
Don Juan.

"Them, too, tonight?" asked Don Juan. "I haven't
given such a successful party in years."

"You still have time to escape, master—listen to
me, take the fastest horse and get out of here!" said
Leporello.

"Are you kidding? With all the money I've spent
on the party? Don't even mention it."

There was really nothing to do. Don Juan's
destiny was to be fulfilled that night, one way or
another. And it would not be Don Juan who got in
its way.

So, little by little, the light of the sun slipped
away from the streets and walls of the city. The

hours and minutes passed, and finally evening came, with the birds wheeling madly in the sky above the squares, and the lamps being lit, one by one, in the streets and in the houses.

Punctually, at sunset, Don Juan entered the great hall of his house, dressed in his richest and most dazzling garments. An enormous table was set, overflowing with flowers, food and wine. Thousands of candles sparkled in the chandeliers, so that from a distance the house seemed to be a fire that had broken out in the heart of the city. The orchestra played, the servants waited, unmoving. Everything was ready.

"Did you leave the front door open, Leporello?" asked Don Juan.

"Just as you ordered, master."

"Good. We have a lot of guests, and I don't want them standing outside."

"But when they arrive, master, what will you say?"

Don Juan had in his eyes the splendour of the room and the marvel of his celebration.

"Long live freedom, I'll say to them. Long live freedom even if it costs you your life. Long live freedom even when it costs the lives of others. Long live freedom, cost what it may."

And just at that moment, through the front door, someone entered the brilliant hall. But the person had no weapons, and it was a woman, extremely elegant, slender and beautiful.

"Donna Elvira!" said Don Juan in amazement. What are you doing here?"

Donna Elvira looked around, smiled, then went up to Don Juan and Leporello. She spoke in a soft, gentle voice.

"They're all out there, Don Juan. It's practically an army. You see how many people want justice,

how many people you've harmed? Is it worthwhile, for a night of pleasure, for the emotion of an evening? I don't know, I can't understand you, but please, at least have the nobility to repent, now, in this last breath of life that remains in you, repent for what you have done, and ask forgiveness from Heaven. Must I imagine you in Hell for all eternity, my love? Don't do this to me, I beg you. You don't have to ask forgiveness from me, or
from any man in the world:
ask forgiveness
from Heaven.

Do it for me, do it for all the women who love you, and who know that you'll soon be dead: at least let them imagine you safe, in some paradise, where your beauty will not be lost. Will you do it?" And she fell on her knees before Don Juan.

Leporello was moved. He looked at his master, and for an instant thought that he really might repent, and ask forgiveness from Heaven. But what Don Juan did was something very different. He leant over, close to Donna Elvira, and placed a kiss on her hair. Then he said to her in a low voice:

"Let me go my own way, my lady. Let me drink and eat and amuse myself, this night. And if you like, stay with me."

Donna Elvira looked up. Then she shook her head no. Her eyes were full of tears. She rose, with wonderful grace. She looked for the last time at Don Juan, then turned and, walking slowly, went out of the hall, and the life of Don Juan, for ever.

Nine

The scene outside the house was really extraordinary. There were the two brothers of Donna Elvira, armed to the teeth and accompanied by their ten swordsmen. But there was also Don Ottavio, and twenty soldiers, led by the chief of police.

The funny thing was that they were quarrelling, because the two brothers claimed to have the right to kill Don Juan first, while the chief of police said that, on the contrary, it was obviously the police who had the right, and the duty, to enter the house first. Don Ottavio proposed that they draw lots, but no one liked that idea, and so they started quarrelling again. They were almost at the point of drawing their swords when they felt the earth tremble under their feet, and heard a strange sound coming closer, like the sound of footsteps, but giant footsteps. They all turned and what they saw was a statue, an enormous white stone statue, slowly approaching, with steps that weighed a ton. Don Ottavio fainted. The chief of police cried "Retreat!" All the soldiers fled, yelling. The ten swordsmen thought that they were not paid enough for a thing like this, and they, too, fled. The two brothers remained.

"It's a trick of Don Juan's," said Don Alfonso, shaking his head.

"If it's a trick, it's very well done," said Don Carlo, and he ran away as fast as he could.

The statue headed directly towards the front door. Don Alfonso stood there, alone. The statue gave him a glance that would have reduced an elephant to ashes. Don Alfonso's hair turned white in an instant. It didn't hurt, but it really was white. "I'm going to faint," he said quietly. And he did.

There was not a living soul around. Only the statue. Which was a dead soul. The dead soul of the Commendatore.

Solemnly it crossed the threshold. It entered the great hall. It was enormous, white, terrifying and purposeful. Don Juan was sitting at the table when he saw it. He had a glass of wine in his hand, and sumptuous food on his plate. "Who would ever have

thought—it really came," he said to himself. The music of the orchestra faded away: the musicians, stunned, had stopped playing. Leporello was hiding under the table. The servants had all fled. Silence. Only the faint squeak of thousands of candles, nothing else.

Don Juan rose. He smiled.

"Welcome, Commendatore," he said. "There's a place at the table for you here, next to me. Sit down."

The statue took a few more steps forwards. Around it everything trembled. When it was in front of Don Juan, it began to speak with its terrifying slowness.

"HE WHO NOW LIVES IN THE HEAVENLY WORLD DOES NOT NOURISH HIMSELF ON MORTAL FOOD."

"I told you," muttered Leporello from under the table. "That thing doesn't eat like us."

"Silence!" shouted Don Juan. And then, addressing the statue, "What can I do for you, then, Commendatore?"

It was incredible, but the statue responded. It really answered.

"YOU INVITED ME TO DINNER AND I

HAVE COME. NOW TELL ME: WILL YOU COME DINE WITH ME?"

"Say no, say no!" shouted Leporello.

But Don Juan leant towards the statue instead. And then he said:

"No one will ever be able to say that I was a coward. I will come and dine with you, Commendatore, you have my word. I will come."

The statue took another step forwards. Then, I swear, it reached out a hand to Don Juan.

"THEN GIVE ME YOUR HAND AS A TOKEN OF YOUR PROMISE," it said.

Leporello slipped out from under the table and, with a cry, fled. That business of the hand was really

too much. Don Juan saw him disappear through the door and said softly, "Farewell, my faithful servant." Then he reached his hand out towards the statue's, and shook it.

He felt a kind of shudder.

"What is this cold?" he murmured. He tried to break free, but the statue's hand crushed his, as in a grip of steel. An inexplicable cold ascended through his arm, and then into his heart, and everywhere. The statue began to shout.

"REPENT, WICKED MAN!"

Don Juan felt his body dying, little by little.

"No," he said, "you will not make me repent for my wonderful life."

"REPENT BEFORE IT'S TOO LATE."

"No!"

"REPENT NOW!"

"No!"

"REPENT I SAY!"

"Go to Hell, you old madman, I will not repent, if it should cost me the Inferno, I will not repent, never!"

He really shouted, with all the voice left in him. "I will not repent, never!"

A terrifying cry arose from the statue, and suddenly the earth gaped beneath Don Juan's feet, and from the enormous chasm the fires of Hell flashed forth, and tongues of flame shot up. Everything plunged into the void, to be destroyed by the flames and the infernal heat, as if swallowed up by a huge, hot throat that had opened up out of nowhere, to devour Don Juan and everything around him. The lavishly laid table disappeared, and then the thousand candles, and the whole hall, and the entire house, until nothing more remained. Then the giant mouth closed again, and carried off the body of Don Juan for ever, along with his black soul. His black, courageous soul.

Epilogue

So ended the life of Don Juan. If you are interested in finding out what happened to the other characters, here's what I know.

Donna Elvira retired to a convent and became a nun: she wanted nothing more to do with men, with love—with anything. Her two brothers lived for a long time, but they were never able to sleep, because every time they closed their eyes that terrible white statue appeared.

Donn'Anna put off her marriage to Don Ottavio, and then put it off again, and then never stopped putting it off: in other words, she never married. So Don Ottavio spent his life waiting, which was, certainly, a thing he knew how to do well. Maybe the only thing. Leporello had to find a new master, but in fact he never did find one because, in comparison to Don Juan, they all seemed terribly boring. In the end he decided to retire to the country. Every so often, at night, he would pick up his former master's catalogue of women and read the names, slowly, as if they were the names of distant lands where it would be wonderful to travel.

As for us, we have never stopped telling this story. We do it, probably, because the adventures of Don Juan hold a question that is important to us, and we don't want to forget it. The question is: are we guilty when fulfilling our desires means others are hurt? Or are our desires always innocent, and is it our right to try to fulfil them? It's not an easy question. You could spend an entire lifetime looking for the answer, in vain. I can only say this: if one day you should happen to find it, let us know.

This book is dedicated to Samuele

WHERE IS THIS
STORY FROM?

The story of Don Juan begins in an obscure, faraway time when people told stories out loud, and death was close, just a breath away from life.

Don Juan may have been a real man—a certain Luis, a priest from Seville who possessed a book for calling up the Devil.

The story was passed on by word of mouth and in the process was transformed, as in a game of Chinese whispers. Finally, in the seventeenth century, a monk named Tirso da Molina had the idea of writing it down and at the same time making it instructive: he called his play *El Burlador de Sevilla* (*The Trickster of Seville*), and it was about a man who murdered another man and went to Hell.

From that moment on the story was wildly successful, and the "rage" for Don Juan lasted for centuries. The story was detached from its dark origins, however, and became a brilliant and at times comic tale: the tale of an irresistible, shameless seducer of women.

Don Juan has been recounted in poetry and music, in every language and dialect.

In Italian theatres it was so popular that even Goldoni staged a version, though he left out walking statues and a floor that cracks open, because he had a thing about realism.

In performances of the *commedia dell'arte*, Don Juan's catalogue was a parchment that was unrolled all the way into the audience, while the Don's servant was often a harlequin character, who also had the ironic names of Fichetto, Ficcanaso and Zuccasecca (Dandy, Busybody and Blockhead).

In France Molière heard about it and in 1665 wrote his own version of the play, in which, by means of Don Juan's lively habits, he was able to make fun of the nobles of the time.

The story of Don Juan had a wide circulation in musical theatre as well.

The very first musical drama was Italian, and was called *L'Empio Punito*. The Princess of Sweden saw it in Rome and was disappointed: evidently she didn't like operas featuring blood and death.

We come upon Don Juan again, a little later, in the eighteenth century, on the night when Mozart, before leaving for Paris, received Molière's play as a gift from his father. Time passed, and Mozart met Lorenzo Da Ponte. Somehow, this meeting produced magic.

For his friend Wolfgang, Lorenzo Da Ponte wrote the libretto for the opera of *Don Giovanni*, which is a true masterpiece. In 1787, along with Mozart's, three other *Don Juan*s appeared. But none succeeded, as Mozart's did, in finding the perfect balance between the comic and the tragic, between Lorenzo and Wolfgang. This was in part because it was a period of freethinkers, and Mozart makes of Don Juan not a man to be punished but a fascinating figure, ready to challenge morality in the name of freedom.

In the past two centuries an essay by the philosopher Kierkegaard, a book by the novelist José Saramago and many films have been devoted to the subject of Don Juan. In one of these Don Juan is a woman, played by the French film star Brigitte Bardot.

The *Don Juan* you have in your hand hopes not to be that one.

The Editor

ALESSANDRO BARICCO is an Italian writer who is read and translated all over the world. He has transformed books into television, and music into books. He knows the stories from the old days and the people of today. He has made a film about someone who very much resembles himself: a professor who has, his entire life, been intent on delivering a mad lecture.

ALESSANDRO MARIA NACAR occupies himself with all that which—in fashion, in advertising, in places—catches his eye. This is his first illustrated book.

ANN GOLDSTEIN is an editor at the *New Yorker*. She has translated works by, among others, Primo Levi, Pier Paolo Pasolini, Alessandro Baricco, Elena Ferrante and Alessandro Piperno, and is currently editing the *Complete Works* of Primo Levi in English. She has been the recipient of several prizes, including a Guggenheim Fellowship, the PEN Renato Poggioli prize and an award from the Italian Ministry of Foreign Affairs.

SAVE THE STORY is a library of favourite stories from around the world, retold for today's children by some of the best contemporary writers. The stories they retell span cultures (from Ancient Greece to nineteenth-century Russia), time and genres (from comedy and romance to mythology and the realist novel), and they have inspired all manner of artists for many generations.

Save the Story is a mission in book form: saving great stories from oblivion by retelling them for a new, younger generation.

THE SCUOLA HOLDEN (Holden School) was born in Turin in 1994. At the School one studies "storytelling", namely the secret of telling stories in all possible languages: books, cinema, television, theatre, comic strips—with extravagant results.

This series is dedicated to Achille, Aglaia, Arturo, Clara, Kostas, Olivia, Pietro, Samuele, Sandra, Sebastiano and Sofia.

PUSHKIN CHILDREN'S BOOKS

Just as we all are, children are fascinated by stories. From the earliest age, we love to hear about monsters and heroes, romance and death, disaster and rescue, from every place and time.

In 2013, we created Pushkin Children's Books to share these tales from different languages and cultures with younger readers, and to open the door to the wide, colourful worlds these stories offer.

From picture books and adventure stories to fairy tales and classics, and from fifty-year-old bestsellers to current huge successes abroad, the books on the Pushkin Children's list reflect the very best stories from around the world, for our most discerning readers of all: children.

For more great stories, visit www.pushkinchildrens.com

SAVE THE STORY: THE SERIES

Don Juan by Alessandro Baricco

Cyrano de Bergerac by Stefano Benni

The Nose by Andrea Camilleri

Gulliver by Jonathan Coe

The Betrothed by Umberto Eco

Captain Nemo by Dave Eggers

Gilgamesh by Yiyun Li

King Lear by Melania G. Mazzucco

Antigone by Ali Smith

Crime and Punishment by A. B. Yehoshua

DATE DUE

			PRINTED IN U.S.A.